PRECISELY INACCURATE

SREELEKHA PABBISETTY

Made with ♥ on the Notion Press Platform
www.notionpress.com

Dedicating this book to my parents, Mr.Pabbisetty Suresh Kumar and Charitha.

Contents

Foreword

A perfect human being is a myth. Everyone has flaws. But what we often do is that we ignore our mistakes and point out others. It doesn't bother us much when we face this with a random person. But if it's with a person with whom the rest of life is destined, it troubles us a lot.

Before getting started with this book, I did profound research where I understood that there are three stages of a relationship. The first stage deals with everything being new and special, where love binds the eyes and people are unaware of their partner's imperfections. The second stage is when they realize each other's positives and negatives. This is where the misunderstandings begin. The final stage is when people accept each other despite knowing each other's negatives. And this is the stage where the real love begins. I started writing a simple and realistic story based on these three stages. While writing the dialogues for each of the characters, I stood in their shoes and put in the effort to make every character look correct from their perspectives. Hence, it gives the reader a feeling of looking at a real-life story happening before their eyes rather than a stage show where the protagonist is completely righteous and the antagonist is entirely wicked. Coming to the question of what a reader learns from the story, I haven't written anything new that this world is not aware of. But it is all about the smallest things in life that people fail to realize, which are, in turn, causing significant problems.

Preface

When I asked my friends to read my previous works, they said they would be reading them if they were novels in the genre of love. They were sure that the genre they had asked me to write in was not my cup of tea. I took it as a challenge to try out a new genre that I had never considered working on. Looking at a relationship from the outside and actually being in a relationship is quite different. Whatever I write remains my understanding of a relationship from the perspective of a person viewing it from the outside. Hence, I had to do a lot of groundwork to make the story look more connected and realistic. On this note, I should be thanking my cousins who had shared their life experiences of being in a relationship. After hearing all their stories, I understood that every relationship is somewhere sharing a standard set of problems. I thought of digging up solutions that are universal yet not acknowledged. Sooner, I started designing the characters of the story in such a way that every couple could relate. I hence thought of writing an adorable love story with a beautiful message.

Acknowledgements

I would like to express my extreme gratitude to God for giving me the strength to write this book. Before starting this novel, I had backstepped several times, fearing my ability to complete it. I believed in God and started the first chapter, after which I have never turned back. I believe that every word I write is just because of the blessings he showers.

I would like to acknowledge the efforts of my Parents, Mr. Pabbisetty Suresh Kumar and Charitha, for giving me a better life. Even if I put their names on the acknowledgments page of all of the books I write, I can't equal the love they share. But this is my small attempt to take a moment to thank them.

Even a rock, when shaped, becomes a beautiful statue. I would like to thank my teachers for helping me become what I'm today.

I would like to thank my sister Sreelaasya for patiently listening to my narration of each chapter.

I should thank my cousins Chitra, Sunil, and Priyanka for giving me free relationship advice which I have used for a few parts of the story.

She is an unhired professional illustrator of mine. It's my friend Adiraju Lakshmi Sowmya, whom I should be thanking for the beautiful illustration in this book.

Thank you, Notionpress.

ONE

MEET AAROHI

'Aarohi, Aarohi.. wait for me. Let's go together,' Sara shouted.

'No way, Sara! I must reach home by the time the tower clock hits 1. I should help mom in the kitchen, bring medicine for dad, have lunch, and return to college by 2:30. So please don't mind Sara. We'll go together in the evening,' Aarohi gently replied.

Aarohi and Sara have been best friends since their childhood. Aarohi is an ambivert and can't quickly mingle with people. Because of this, she doesn't have a good number of friends. She has a younger brother and a younger sister who are twins. Since they are twins, they prefer bonding with each other rather than Aarohi. She got used to a lonely life for a very long time now. The sole companion she has is Sara. Sara is the only one with whom she shares everything. Aarohi is shy to make new connections. But once she befriends anyone, she becomes dearer to them. She is insecure about revealing herself to the world. Apart from this, she is good at heart. She is generous and compassionate. She is simple and obedient.

As soon as Aarohi reached home, her mom gave a shocker to her. 'Look, Aarohi, It's high time you quit college and help me at home. Your father is not feeling well and is unable to maintain the shop. I am fed up with managing the shop and the household alone. We need your help running this house.'

'But mom..' Aarohi paused for a second.

'No more discussions on it. Do what I said. Your dad and I have been managing this house. But now your dad is not healthy enough to do it as before. Nothing is more important than your dad's health. You should help the family at hard times,' Aarohi's mom sharply said.

Aarohi went to her room and stood before the mirror.

'No one is interested in my opinions. No one is bothered about my future. I am just born to follow orders. I don't even have the right to make decisions in my own life. I have my interests and views. But who cares? I am not even allowed to express my opinions. Anyways, even if I am given a chance to express myself, I can't dare to oppose their decisions. Feeling pity for myself. Poor Aarohi, Your life is out of your hands,' She spoke to herself in grief.

In the evening, Sara came to Aarohi's home and started yelling in resentment. 'Wow, Aarohi! You said we would come together in the evening. And you didn't even show up at the college after lunch. I had to come alone.'

'Please stop picking a fight, Sara. I am not in the mood,' Aarohi replied in disappointment.

'Hey! What happened, Aaru?' Sara inquired.

'Mom asked me to quit college and help her with the household. I won't be coming to college further. And I can't make out to meet you frequently. You have to go to college all alone from now on,' Aarohi expressed her anguish.

'I am very sorry, Aaru. I didn't know what you were going through. Let me talk to your mom about this,' Sara expressed solicitude.

'Aunty, Can I talk to you for a second?' Sara asked Aarohi's mom.

'Ah! Please, Sara. If you want to talk about Aarohi attending college, You are wasting your time. I will not change my decision,' Aarohi's mom said firmly.

'What is this, Aaru? I already told you that I would not change my decision on this. Now, why did you bring your friend in support? I won't change my decision even if your dad asks me to,' Aarohi's mom added.

After this conversation, Aarohi lost hope of attending college and finishing her education. She can neither oppose her mom nor change her mind. She landed in a tight spot. But as she couldn't dare do anything against her parent's will, she slowly started convincing herself to get adjusted to the new normal. Let's see what's in store for Aarohi in the future.

TWO

PRANAV'S WORLD

Pranav is an extrovert. He is enthusiastic and outgoing. His activeness in social gatherings is always appreciated. No matter what the event is. He loves to be a part of it. He is amiable and talkative. He maintains a vast circle of friends. He is well-known for his benevolence. He lost his father when he was 18. He used to live with his mother, Ratna, and his sister Krishna. Krishna was recently married to Bhushan and is now a housewife. Pranav completed his graduation and got into his family business. He is working hard to bring back the glory to their business. Though he is too young for that particular field of work, he is responsible enough to run the business smoothly. As he is not a professional, he faces challenges but never gives up on them. The only downside is that he quickly gets manipulated at times. He is not confident enough to stick to his decisions.

One day, Krishna came to her mom's home on the eve of a local festival. 'Mom, I'm home!!' Krishna shouted in excitement.

'Welcome, welcome, my little princess. Where is your husband? Didn't he come along with you?' Ratna inquired.

'He is busy with his work, mom. He asked me to go alone,' Krishna replied.

'You could have brought him. This festival is special, Krishna. Isn't it? People from different parts of the state come to witness the grandeur of our local festival. But my son-in-law is busy working,' Ratna spoke in distress.

'Mom, I am right in front of you. Instead of feeling happy, you are worried about your son-in-law. This is not fair, mom. If you continue doing this, I'll go back,' Krishna bemoaned.

'Alright! Go and refresh yourself. Evening we have a stage show in our street. We'll have to be there at least an hour before. Or else we won't get a place in the front row,' Ratna sighed.

'Ok, mom. I am tired of the journey. Let me take some rest. By the way, where is Pranav? I haven't seen him since I came home,' Krishna asked.

'He has gone out with his friends. He might be here anytime,' Ratna replied.

That evening, Ratna and Krishna went to the stage show. As soon as they reached the venue, Ratna started yelling in annoyance. 'It's all because of you, Krishna. We would have come a bit early If you weren't late. Look! We could hardly see the stage now.'

Meanwhile, Krishna spotted something and began shouting in astonishment. 'Mom! Look, Who it is. It's our Pranav performing in the stage show. Wow, Pranav! Go on.'

'He didn't even tell me that he was going to perform. What a boy he is. He doesn't share anything with me,' Ratna expressed displeasure.

'Come on, Mom. Stop taunting him. Look at his grace. Enjoy his show,' Krishna said in a pleasing tone.

After the show, Pranav joined his mom and sister on their way home. 'Mom, How was my show?' Pranav asked out of curiosity.

'Umm. It was nice. But it could have been nicer if you had told me before,' Ratna replied.

'It wasn't planned, mom. This morning they called me and asked if I could play a role. I said yes. Since there was less time, I had to stay and practice until the evening. And I thought I would surprise you,' Pranav justified his actions.

'Don't give such surprises, Pranav. It's always good that you share anything with your sister or me before we know it from someone else. Anyways, all our neighbors were praising your performance. I felt happy to hear them. But remember! Next time, you should tell me beforehand,' Ratna concisely advised.

Pranav nodded his head as a sign of acceptance. Krishna and Pranav looked at each other and laughed in silence.

Pranav always behaves as if he follows every instruction of his mother. But deep inside, he has his plans. He doesn't want to hurt anyone. At the same time, he wants to do whatever he wishes to. Hence, he plays smart in front of his mom. As Ratna loves Pranav so much, She forgives him all the time.

THREE

A MATCH MADE IN HEAVEN

Aarohi is tense. She is running towards the examination hall. Time is running out. She is doing her last-minute revision. The bell has been ringing. Everyone is rushing into the exam hall. Aarohi is sweating and is in a hurry. The invigilator is forcing her to enter the hall.

All of a sudden, Aarohi screamed and woke up from her dream.

'What is it, Aarohi? Why is that scream?' Aarohi's mom was concerned.

'It was a nightmare, mom. I dreamt that I was rushing to an exam hall and was pressurized at the last minute,' Aarohi spoke in restlessness.

'Your dreams are a manifestation of your thoughts, Aarohi. It has been a year since you discontinued your studies. But still, you are getting dreams regarding the same. It means you are still stuck at the same point. Learn to move on in your life,' her mom advised.

On the other hand, Krishna gently started a conversation with Pranav.

'It was a fantastic stage show, Pranav. You lived in character. I mean it.'

'Umm, what's the matter, Krishna?'

'Ah, nothing!'

'See Krishna. I know that you would never praise me for no reason. You would need something in return. Am I right?'

'Correct Guess, Kiddo! But, This time, I want....'

'Wait! Now don't ask me to buy that make-up kit. A minimal makeover itself makes you feel like a movie actress. If I buy you a new one, You will be over the moon.'

'Stop making fun of me, Pranav. I am serious.'

'Okay, ma'am! Tell me what you would want.'

'Dang! Have some seriousness in your life, Pranav. All your friends are getting married. I want you too to get married.'

'So! This time you came home with an agenda. But let me tell you something. You already know the situation of our family, right? After dad left us, There were so many debts, and income was insufficient. There was no one to help me here. People gave me suggestions on quitting the existing business and starting something new. But I wanted to continue dad's legacy after him. I knew nothing about our business, but I have never given up on it. After struggling hard, now, I am settling into the business. I don't want to speed up things. I need some time, Krishna.'

'I appreciate your accountability, Pranav. But remember that you should do the right thing at the right time. It's time to marry Pranav. It's time you get a better half. You certainly need someone to share your heart with. How long will you stay alone? Put a full stop to your loneliness and welcome new beginnings.'

'Well, I'll think of it sometime later.'

'You should think about it right away. I already have someone in my mind.'

'Does mom know about all these?'

'Yeah. I already spoke to her.'

'Mmm... So it's preplanned, is it?'

Krishna smiled.

'Who is it on your mind, Krishna? Is it someone I already knew?'

'Nah! I went to my friend's place for her wedding almost a year ago. I saw a girl telling her friend that she must reach home early as she would have to help her parents. I saw a sense of responsibility in her, Pranav. I saw you in her. She is as responsible as you are. I thought you both would make a good pair. I asked my friend to get her details. After going through her details, I learned that she was studying. So I didn't want to make a wedding proposal that soon. But recently, I got to know that she had discontinued her education the very day I saw her. She quit her education to help her parents, it seems. Nowadays, it's hard to find such girls, Pranav. Also, it's rare to find a good guy like my brother. So I feel it's a match made in heaven.'

'Did you speak with her parents then?'

'I had an initial talk, Pranav. But you have to talk to them further. If dad were there, he would have taken care of it. Now, you have to handle this yourself. Call them immediately and ask for a possible date to meet and discuss.'

'Why are you making it too early, Krishna?'

'We have to make it fast before someone else asks her out for marriage.'

'Ok, Krishna! Let me call them now. What is her dad's name?'

'He is Mr.Narayan.'

Pranav started making a call to the girl's dad.

'Hello! Am I speaking to Mr. Narayan?' Pranav inquired.

'Sorry! I am his daughter. Dad just went out. Is it anything important? Do you want me to convey anything to him?' Aarohi asked.

'Ah! Ok, so my sister spoke to your dad regarding a wedding proposal. We are planning to come to your home to talk about it. Ask your dad to fix a feasible date and let us know about the same,' Pranav answered.

Aarohi was awe-struck.

Pranav firmly pressed the receiver against the phone.

'Shhh! Why are you pressing it so hard?' Krishna asked Pranav.

As Ratna was passing by them, She heard Krishna. 'What should I say about this phone, Krishna? For namesake, we are the first family in our town to have a landline connection. But this phone is not at all working properly. Calls are not getting disconnected until and unless we press it so hard. Many things are troubling me, Krishna. And this phone is one among them,' Ratna sighed.

Back at Aarohi's home, It took nearly 10 minutes for her to realize what had just happened. She went to her mom and talked about the phone conversation.

'Oh! Is it? I will talk to your dad about this,' her mom said.

'Mom, Do you already know about this proposal?' Aarohi was startled.

'Yes, dear! Your dad spoke to me about this,' her mom replied.

'Mom, so why didn't you tell me before?' she muttered.

'I completely understand you, Aarohi. Initially, we didn't have any plans regarding your wedding. They saw you somewhere, it seems. They only approached us. Morally and financially, they are good, it seems. Anyways you had quit college, and now even your dad got recovered. Why being idle at home, Aarohi? If not today, at least tomorrow, we would have started planning your wedding. So we thought we should consider their proposal,‘ her mom detailed.

Aarohi's face seemed to have a lot of questions. Even before she could ask something, her mom tried comforting her. 'Look, Aarohi! Though we didn't plan anything, everything is happening one after another. So, it seems to be God's plan. Don't worry and relax. God's plan will always be the best one. Trust me. Maybe it's a match made in heaven.'

FOUR

LOVE AT FIRST FIGHT?

"Aarohi, her name is," Krishna said.

"I didn't ask," Pranav replied.

"I know. The match is almost confirmed. But we don't even have the girl's picture. At least you better know her name before we reach their home," said Krishna.

"By the way, Where is your husband? Is he going to join us? Or is he still busy with his work?" Pranav asked Krishna.

"He said he would come directly to the girl's hometown. There is a famous temple over there. I asked him to join us from there. We have to reach before he does. If we have to reach early, we have to stop talking now and start immediately," Krishna was playful.

"You only started the conversation, but now you are acting as if I am the one making the delay," Pranav was provoked.

Krishna laughed at him.

"Now, both of you, stop your stupid fight and get into the car," Ratna yelled.

Ratna, Krishna, and Pranav started to Aarohi's hometown.

After a couple of hours, Aarohi's mom Chandra was very busy with the arrangements.

"I should only take care of everything. No one in this house is interested in helping me out. Is it necessary for these two kids to go to school today? It is the first wedding in our home. We should not neglect even the smallest formalities," Chandra was tense.

"Relax, Chandra! It's just the first meeting," Naryan tried comforting her.

"You are all men. You don't care about formalities. But people from the groom's side observe everything. We should be perfect on our part," Chandra added.

"Look, Chandra! I've already inquired about the groom. He is a very good person, it seems. They are not the people who feel bad for every minute thing," Narayan sounded confident.

"If something goes wrong, I'll be the one to be blamed. So I can't take a chance," Chandra moaned.

"Are you ready, Aaru? We have to go to the temple and should be back by the time they reach our home," Chandra shouted.

"Yeah, Mom. I am ready. Let's go," said Aarohi.

Narayan, Chandra, and Aarohi went to the temple.

Three of them were in the queue, but because of the heavy crowd, Aarohi was slightly behind.

"Aaru, don't worry. We are here waiting for you. Let the queue move, and you can join us," Chandra shouted.

"Ok, mom!" said Aarohi, and she closed her eyes. She started praying to God.

"Dear God, I realized that nothing is in my hands. I am surrendering myself to you. I believe in you. I abide by your decisions. Please give me strength."

Meanwhile, someone from behind stepped on Aarohi's dupatta. She furiously turned back.

"Excuse me!" She called out.

"Yes," Pranav replied.

"Can't you see?" She bitterly spoke.

"I can see. I am not blind," Pranav naively answered back.

"Not funny. Can you just...." Aarohi kept blustering at Pranav.

But Pranav wasn't paying attention to her words. He was concentrating only on her voice. "I am sure that I have heard this voice before. But where did I hear? Umm...Let me recollect," he spoke in his mind.

"Hello! I am talking to you. Should I beg you further?" Aarohi vented out her anger.

"Why are you shouting like this? I am also a human like you. And I'm not deaf. You can lower your tone," Pranav boldly reacted.

"I am shouting because you are not paying attention to me. Now, Kindly remove your foot off my dupatta," She restrained.

"Oh! I am very sorry. I didn't notice," Pranav immediately apologized and moved his leg off it.

Krishna was standing behind Pranav and was talking to her husband, Bhushan. While Pranav was apologizing to Aarohi, Krishna looked ahead to see who he was talking to. Soon Krishna realized that it was Aarohi. She immediately asked Pranav to move a bit and came in front.

Pranav observed Krishna's eagerness and began whispering in her ear. "Sshh! Krishna, It's my mistake. I said sorry too. Everything is fine. Now don't rebuke her."

"Shut up, Kiddo!" Krishna laughed.

"How are you.. Aarohi?" Krishna asked her.

Pranav got stunned and looked at Aarohi.

"Do.. I.. know you?" Aarohi wondered.

"No. But I know you. We are the ones who approached your family with a wedding proposal," Krishna said.

"Oh, I didn't know that it was you. I am good. How about you?" She asked Krishna and looked at Pranav.

"I'm good. And he is my brother, Pranav. He is the groom," Krishna smiled and introduced Pranav to Aarohi.

Meanwhile, the queue moved, and Krishna asked Aarohi about the latter's parents.

"They are waiting for me in the front," She answered.

As soon as they reached her parents, everyone introduced themselves to each other. After having the darshan, they all got to the temple's main gate.

"Our home is nearby. We will go walking. You can follow us in your vehicle," Chandra said.

"Oh! If it's that near, then let's go together. We'll also join you on the walk," Krishna said.

On their way home, Aarohi was embarrassed about her act and wasn't even raising her head.

"Have I overreacted? I shouldn't have behaved like that. He might think that I am very aggressive. People say that the first impression becomes the best one. But I spoiled everything," She regretfully spoke in her mind.

Pranav understood the situation and tried comforting her. "Well, You didn't do anything wrong. You have been the way everyone deals with a stranger."

Aarohi was listening and didn't raise her head.

"You can feel free to talk to me," Pranav further tried to make her comfortable.

But she still didn't raise her head.

"Is anyone paying you for not raising your head?" Pranav satirically added.

"What?" She raised her head.

Pranav laughed.

"Should I laugh at his joke? Is this a joke, first of all? He might feel bad if I don't laugh. Ah! It won't be nice if I laugh after this long time. I should stay quiet for now," She spoke in her mind.

"This is our home," Chandra introduced.

"Oh! So it is too near to the temple," Krishna said.

"Yeah," Chandra replied.

Many of us judge a person on the first meeting and end up with an opinion about them. If that opinion is 'good', whatever they do seems good to us. If it's 'bad', we hate them for no reason. But Pranav didn't judge Aarohi based on one single situation. He reviewed the situation from her perspective and concluded that Aarohi's emotion in that particular scenario was valid. In addition, he stepped forward to help her evade discomfort.

FIVE

WEDDING BELLS?

All of them went into the home. Bhushan asked Pranav to come aside and began enquiring about something. 'Erm...I don't know how to begin. Before proceeding with the wedding discussion, let me ask you something. What do you think about the dowry?'

'Ah! I'm fine even if they don't offer anything,' Pranav answered.

'You shouldn't say that, Pranav. Once the wedding gets fixed, everyone starts asking about the dowry. We should ask the girl's parents for a reasonable sum so that we can maintain our status in society. I should be the one representing our family in the wedding discussion. So I am taking at most care about protecting our family's reputation. Think about it. We are not asking them for dowry just for the sake of us. It would also become a matter of pride for them,' Bhushan said.

'Okay. I agree with your decision. You take care of the rest,' Pranav admitted Bhushan's words.

Bhushan went on to Mr.Narayan to finalize the wedding. 'Before getting to a conclusion about the wedding, We have a request from our side.'

'What is it about?' Narayan questioned with uncertainty.

'We'll take care of your daughter more than how you did. We just want you to afford only the dowry,' Bhushan spoke to Narayan.

'Dowry? Sorry, but... You might have known our financial status. I cannot afford the dowry,' Narayan replied politely.

'Our Pranav is a perfect guy and settled in his life. We got many wedding proposals from many people. But we preferred only yours. I agree that we only approached you, but it doesn't mean we would do his wedding without a dowry. We are very serious about it. We don't want to lessen his stature by not taking anything,' Bhushan firmly spoke.

'We can not afford them. Let's quit the discussion here,' Chandra implied to Narayan.

'Wait, Chandra! Let me take some time and think of it,' Narayan responded.

'It's time to decide whether to move forward with the wedding proceedings or stop it here. But if the match gets fixed, your daughter's life will be hassle-free,' Bhushan stressed his intentions.

Narayan lowered his head and didn't utter even a word. He felt dejected.

Chandra understood his pain and thought of convincing him. 'See, they are making it clear. They wouldn't be stepping back from their decision. We should drop off their proposal right here. Let's not make it complex. We have two more kids. We have to take care of their lives as well'.

'I don't want to miss this proposal,' Narayan murmured.

'There are so many people. We could get an even better groom in the future. Why are you so adamant?' Chandra was furious.

'Why lose a good one now and wait for another good one in the future? We are not sure whether another groom in the future would ask for a dowry or not. And one more thing. When you asked Aarohi to quit her education, She did it right away just for the sake of our family. I felt sad as she wasn't able to finish her education. We didn't give her a good career. At least let us try to give her a good life,' Narayan spoke regretfully.

'Do whatever you wish,' Chandra fumed in rage.

'Ok, But I need some time to pay you,' Narayan took some time and responded to Bhushan.

'Okay, But you should do it before we start the wedding proceedings. Call us whenever you are ready with the dowry, and we will start the procedures the next day,' Bhushan was persistent.

Aarohi's parents were in a discussion about the arrangement of the dowry amount.

'We have our money in Mr.Rao's chit fund, right? We should ask him for it,' said Narayan.

In the meantime, Bhushan went to Pranav and said that the wedding had been fixed.

'Oh, Is it? Okay,' Pranav was delighted inside but wasn't expressing himself. He went out immediately.

Bhushan spoke to Ratna and Krishna regarding the confirmation of the wedding. Krishna was very joyful and was sharing her plans for Pranav's wedding. Everyone's busy with their discussions. Pranav returned with a gift pack and began a conversation with Aarohi.

'You can now fight with me for the rest of your life,' he said.

Aarohi had a question mark on her face.

'A small gift for you,' he offered her the gift he brought.

Aarohi was reluctant to accept it.

'You can take it. Our wedding had been fixed,' Pranav made it clear.

Aarohi was a little tense and a little sad. She was tense being in a new atmosphere. She was sad as she could no longer help her parents, and they would have to work harder in her absence. After a while, she accepted Pranav's gift and opened it.

'It's a ring. I don't know the exact measurement, but I made a guess. Is it fitting well?' he asked.

'Um,' She nodded her head.

'It was better when we were strangers. You spoke more with me then,' he bantered and laughed.

'It isn't anything like that. I couldn't quickly mingle with people,' Aarohi muttered.

'We should travel together for our entire life. We should start getting to know each other. Feel comfortable,' Pranav said.

'Tell me about yourself. What are your interests? What do you do,' he added after a couple of minutes.

'I lead a very normal life. Managing my studies and helping my family used to be my daily routine. But now...,' She paused.

'Now?' he inquired.

'You might have known that I discontinued my education,' She said.

'Yeah, I know,' Pranav replied.

'Can I ask you something?' he asked after a pause.

'Yeah,' She replied.

'Why are you hesitant to mingle with people?' he questioned.

'If I get closer to people, they will get to know about my positives and negatives. After knowing everything, I am scared they might take advantage of me. I become closer only if I feel secure and comfortable,' She answered.

'You can share anything with me. But as you said, only when I create a ray of trust in you,' he assured.

Aarohi looked into his eyes and immediately lowered her eyes. 'Did he just give me space? How endearing! Did I start liking him? Or.. is he being too lovable?' She spoke in her mind.

'Ok, we will take a leave now. Our son-in-law Bhushan will contact you with further proceedings,' Ratna spoke to Narayan.

Pranav heard his mother and turned towards Aarohi. 'Okay, I'll take a leave now. Longing to start new beginnings with you.'

SIX

Blessing or a Curse?

'Aaru... The phone has been ringing. Pick it up,' Chandra shouted.

Aarohi picked up the call.

'Hello, Who is it?' She asked.

'Guess who it is.'

'Guess?' She paused.

'Ok, I know who it is,' She added.

'Then tell me,' he was curious.

'Who is it on the phone, Aaru?' Chandra asked Aarohi.

'It's Pranav, mom,' She replied.

'Oh,' Chandra continued with her work.

'Finally, my name came out of your mouth. Thus, it became the luckiest name ever.'

'Hmm...Your sister already told me.'

'My sister? What did she tell you?'

'She said that you are a magician of words. She also said that you manipulate your mom with your smartness. Therefore, she asked me not to fall for your words.'

'What? I follow my heart. All the words that I speak are from my heart. Wait... When did Krishna tell you all these? I haven't seen both of you talking that day.'

'You went out to get a gift, right? In the meantime, Krishna came to me and shared her excitement regarding our wedding. In her flow, She talked about all this.'

'Ooh. So it means you already knew about the wedding, even before I told you. But you have acted as if I am the first person talking to you about the wedding.'

Aarohi swiftly closed her eyes as a sign of getting caught. She felt shy to speak a word.

'Okay So now tell me who is smart,' Pranav smiled.

Meanwhile, Ratna was passing by Pranav.

'Whom are you talking to, Pranav?' Ratna inquired.

'It's my friend "Giri", mom,' he lied without hesitation.

'Um, now tell me who acts smart,' Aarohi laughed.

'Ok, ok. Both of us are. But let me tell you something,' he halted for a second.

Aarohi stopped laughing.

'It's nice that you are being comfortable with me,' he added.

Aarohi realized that she had mingled well with him without her notice.

'Ah! Ok, I have to look after the shop. Dad just went out,' She hung up the call immediately and smiled.

Pranav looked at the receiver and laughed.

Post noon, the very same day, Aarohi heard a few sounds. She slowly stepped towards the living room. She saw her mom inquiring about her dad being upset.

'Mr. Bhushan called me and asked us to join them for wedding shopping tomorrow,' Narayan said. His eyes were wet, and his voice was shivering.

'Tomorrow?' Chandra asked.

'He said he would be busy later. Also, He indirectly asked me to bring the dowry money.'

'How do we arrange money in this short span? Yeah! We thought of asking Mr. Rao regarding our chit-fund money, right?'

'Chandra, I already went to him. Even after telling him the need for the money, he said he can't give the money right away.'

'Your brothers? They owe us money, right?'

'They said they can give me only minimal amounts as of now. The money they said they would give doesn't add any value to the dowry.'

'You could have borrowed money from your friends.'

'I tried that as well. I kept my self-respect aside and went on to ask them. I got to know that Mr. Rao circulated to the entire town that I went to him for chit-fund money. He has been telling everyone that I am not able to afford the money, even for my daughter's wedding. So whomever I asked turned down my request, fearing that I might not pay them back,' Narayan expressed his extreme grief and was just staring at the floor. He was crestfallen.

'Is it this hard to give a proper life to my girl, Chandra?' he questioned and sobbed.

Tears rolled out of Aarohi's eyes. 'Dowry? Isn't it a crime? Besides the wedding expenses, if they expect a dowry, how do we afford it? Should a father's life be turned upside down for his girl's wedding?' She spoke in her mind.

Suddenly, a thought struck her mind. 'Dad,' She slowly called out.

'What are you doing here, Aaru?' Chandra asked.

'I'll just come, Mom,' She said and went to her almirah. She came back and stood before Narayan. Narayan slowly raised his head and looked at Aarohi.

'Take this, dad,' Aarohi placed the cover she brought in his hand.

'What is this?' he inquired.

'The dowry amount,' She replied.

Before Narayan could ask, She began telling him how she got the money. 'Right from my childhood, I had been observing that we do not have any savings. Whatever we earn has been going the way it came. I feared this situation prior. For the last few years, I have saved fewer amounts of money daily from our shop. And today, the money I have been collecting has become huge. I agree that I shouldn't be doing it without your notice. But still, I feel it is correct, keeping in mind our financial condition. Take this, dad,' She concluded.

For the next few minutes, the hall was filled with silence. None of them uttered a single word. Chandra switched her looks from Aarohi to Narayan. She slowly patted with her palm on Narayan's shoulder.

'Aaru...' Narayan cried out, holding her hands.

'It's indeed a wise decision. You are a savior today,' he wiped his tears off. But still, the flow of his tears didn't stop.

'Now, Now... I will call and tell them that we are ready with the money. Aaru, my dear...Your wedding will now happen without any obstacles,' he added with tears of contentment.

Three of them were relieved and happy.

Later that day, Sara came to Aarohi's home.

'What's the matter, Miss. Bride?' Sara teased Aarohi.

'Thank God! You are here today. I hardly need someone to share my thoughts with,' Aarohi started conversing with Sara.

'I know! I am an almighty. Hence, I will appear in front of your eyes as soon as you think of me,' Sara was playful.

'Hmmm...Nice, Now stop your senseless statements and listen to me,' Aarohi sighed.

'Ha! Tell me. So, Your life had a turn just in the last two weeks. How does all of this make you feel?' Sara was anxious.

'It's been a roller coaster ride, Sara. I am unsure whether these new beginnings are a blessing or a curse. I don't know how the rest of my life is destined. I hope whatever is happening is happening for the sake of good,' said, Aarohi.

'How was your fiance's family? Are they being nice to you?' Sara questioned.

Aarohi was quiet for a while.

'I am confused, Sara. At first, they all seemed good. Later...' She paused.

'I know. I've heard of it, Aaru. Uncle was worried about dowry, it seems, right? My dad was talking about it when he came for lunch. Remember one thing, Aaru. Don't allow your worries to conquer your happy moments. There might be several circumstances that would be trying to interrupt your relationship with Pranav. But at the end of the day, he is the one with whom you should lead your life. Don't let all those circumstances create a gap between both of you. Problems come and go. But if you allow those problems to pierce your relationship, you might lose people,' Sara advised.

Aarohi held Sara's hands and took a deep breath.

'I'm thankful to you, Sara,' Aarohi smiled.

SEVEN

GAME ON!

As per Bhushan's plan, both families met each other for the wedding shopping. Narayan's face was filled with pride and confidence. Pranav looked at Aarohi and smiled, but she didn't react. Ratna and Chandra were inquiring about each other's whereabouts.

"Hmm...So, you are feeling insecure," Pranav spoke to Aarohi.

"Ah! No," She said.

"It's quite evident. Whenever our families meet, I can see you face discomfort. It's pretty usual to feel uneasy being around new people," he said and paused.

"So, Tell me, how are you?" He tried distracting her.

"We just spoke yesterday. You might have known how I am," She looked at him.

"But it feels like ages," he said.

"Not again!" Aarohi laughed.

"Ok, Ok! Which is your favorite color? And which color suits you well?" he asked.

"Umm... I like yellow. And you only tell me which color would suit me," she asked.

"Maybe green might suit you," he suggested.

After hearing him, she said 'okay' but started thinking about choosing a green saree. "Green? I don't think it would look good on me. But since he is suggesting something, for the first time, Let me choose something green. But I don't think he has good taste. Ok, how will he even know? He might be unsure of sarees and color combinations," She spoke in her mind.

"Aarohi... What are you thinking of?" he called her as she paused.

"Nothing. I'm just thinking of choosing a green saree."

"Oh, so the one I suggested. Now tell me this. Did you like me? Or was it forceful?" he asked out of curiosity.

Aarohi suddenly looked at him as he instantly changed the topic from generic to specific. After a deep pause, she began telling him. "Initially, I was scared and worried. I felt everything happening all of a sudden. I took time... and later, after talking to you a couple of times, I accepted the reality."

"You had to accept the reality? So, it means was it forceful?" he asked.

"No, no, I didn't mean," she said.

"What didn't you mean?" he asked.

"I do..." she tried pleasing him.

"You do? What do you do?" he asked.

"I do like you," she said in a flow.

"Oh...Is it?" He looked into her eyes and stressed his words.

She turned her face away from him, closed her eyes with her hand, and smiled. "Why am I getting caught all the time?" she questioned herself.

"Pranav.." Krishna called him.

"This is the saree shop I was talking about. The men's store is a bit far from here. You go along with Bhushan,"

Krishna guided Pranav.

"Come, Aarohi! Let's begin our shopping," Krishna called her.

Aarohi looked at Pranav. He moved his head as a sign of saying 'bye'. All of them were busy shopping for their sarees. Chandra and Ratna sat together. Krishna and Aarohi sat next to them.

"Krishna, the wedding has been fixed for the 3rd of next month. We should soon start with the wedding card distribution. Ask Bhushan for his leisure time so that he can join us," said Ratna.

"Sure, Mom. I'll ask him and let you know," Krishna replied.

Soon, they finished shopping and were waiting for the shopkeeper to pack the sarees. In the meantime, Krishna started a conversation with Aarohi.

"Nice bangles, Aarohi!" She gave a compliment.

"Thank you," Aarohi smiled.

"And this ring. It is too good. Where did you buy this?" Krishna asked.

"Pranav gifted this to me," said Aarohi.

Ratna and Krishna looked at each other with blankness on their faces. They then looked at Aarohi's ring. After that, they didn't utter even a word. Aarohi identified oddness in their behavior. But she didn't ask them anything.

Krishna and Bhushan started to their native.

"According to our tradition, the groom should finish a few formalities at our home before the wedding. Please send him when he is free," Narayan asked Ratna.

"Hmm," Ratna sighed.

Pranav and Aarohi bid goodbye to each other and started to their hometowns.

After reaching home, Pranav was talking to Ratna. "Mom, It would have been nice if Krishna had come with us, right?"

Ratna was angry at him and hence wasn't answering him.

"Mom.. I am talking to you," Pranav increased his tone.

"I didn't know that you had grown this older, Pranav. You are making your own decisions. Just because you are getting married doesn't mean you can do whatever you wish," She expressed displeasure.

"What did I do, mom? All of a sudden, you are blaming me for no reason. At least tell me the reason and then shout at me," he was confused.

"Oh, My grief seems like a scream to you. Is it? Now you are asking me about what you did. Did you even bother to ask any of us before presenting a ring to her?" She opened up.

Pranav's face was out of expression. He was just looking at Ratna. Deep inside, he was tense.

"Mom, I thought of telling you in advance. But..." before he could say something, Ratna interrupted him. "Now, don't try to outsmart me, Pranav. I had to know about the happenings in my home from an outside girl."

"Aarohi?" he said in his mind.

He tried convincing his mom. But nothing worked. Ratna wasn't even willing to pay attention to his words. On the next day, he made a call to Aarohi.

"Hello, Who is it?" asked Aarohi's sister.

"Is Aarohi there?"

"Before I give the phone to her, tell me who you are."

"It's Pranav here."

"Oh... But Aarohi is not at home."

"When will she come home?"

"She will come to your home on the 3rd of next month," She teased him and laughed.

Pranav was enraged.

Before he could say anything, she started speaking.

"Aarohi hasn't gone anywhere. She is at home. Just a second. I'll give it to her," She still didn't stop laughing.

Pranav tried controlling his anger. After a few seconds, he heard a voice from the receiver.

"Hello, Pranav?" Aarohi inquired.

"Yeah, It's Pranav here."

Aarohi identified anger in his tone.

"Is everything fine?" she asked.

"No."

"What happened?"

"Let me ask you something, Aarohi. Did you tell my mom that I've presented a ring to you?"

"Yeah...But.. what happened?"

"Why did you tell everyone about it? If there is something between us, it should remain between us. You are disrupting privacy. I didn't tell my mom about it. Unnecessarily you have now spoken about it," he fumed in anger.

"How would I know that you hide things from your mom, Pranav? There would be no secrets between my parents and me. I share everything with them. I don't even know that people hide such things from their parents. You could have told me before not to reveal the ring to your family," she said in a state of nervousness.

"How would I know that you would not be aware of even the simplest things?" He was livid.

Aarohi was blank for a second. She then put off the receiver and was in despair. Pranav furiously put down the receiver.

Sometimes in a fight, there would be no question of who is correct and who is wrong. Both of them would be correct in their perspectives. In such cases, if a person thinks from the other person's viewpoint, it might immediately end the misunderstandings.

EIGHT

BATTLE OF EGOS!

"What is this, Krishna? We don't have much time for the wedding. You should have been here and helped me out. Even last week, after finishing the shopping, you went to your hometown. It would have been nice if you had accompanied us that day. Even Pranav was talking about the same," Ratna was speaking to Krishna on the phone.

"Even I feel like coming home, Mom. I'm eager to take part in all of his wedding arrangements. I'll talk to Bhushan and probably start tomorrow," said Krishna.

"And what about Bhushan? When would he be here? We thought of starting with the wedding cards distribution, right?" Ratna asked.

"He will probably join a couple of days later, mom," Krishna answered in a pleasing tone.

"Who is it, Mom? Is that Krishna on the call?" Pranav inquired.

"Yeah, Pranav. She is telling me that she will be starting tomorrow," Ratna answered.

Right after Krishna reached home the next day, She rushed everyone into working on the wedding arrangements.

"Ah! Pranav, I've made a list. Go and get these immediately," Krishna hurried him.

"You just came, Krishna. Do take time and give time to me," Pranav was a little rude.

"Don't you want me to make your wedding arrangements? Or didn't you like me coming home? You already knew that I was coming, right?" She was confused.

"It's not about you, Krishna. I'm not in the mood to do all these," he said.

"You are not in the mood to make your wedding arrangements. So it is either a problem with your wedding or a problem with the bride. Is it?" Krishna inquired.

Pranav was quiet with his head lowered.

"Are terms good between you and Aarohi?" She asked.

Pranav suddenly looked at Krishna.

"Hence, Proved. Something is going on between both of you. Is there a mistake from her side?" She asked.

"Mistakes are from my side, too," he sighed.

"Then go and apologize."

"What? Should I go and beg her for forgiveness?"

"I don't know what happened between both of you. But let me tell you something. When you both met in the temple for the first time, when you both were strangers, you weren't hesitant to apologize to her right after realizing your mistake. Now you both are far more than strangers. She is your better half. Now you are stepping back to say sorry. Why does your ego grow as you grow dearer to a person?"

"Ego? It's easy to preach, Krishna. But it's harder to put it into practice. In the case of strangers, we would not have met after apologizing. But now, she would have a point to put me down for the rest of my life. I don't want to give her that chance. I'm not ready to kneel before a girl younger than me."

"This. I'm talking exactly about this, Pranav. This is what is called ego. It's basic to say sorry to a human with whom you dealt wrong. Before treating her as your fiance or a girl younger than you, treat her as a human. It's better that she takes a chance on your apologies rather than you living with the guilt. You don't need to kneel and say sorry. Let your actions speak. Everything will settle down. Do as I said."

"I'll think of it, Krishna."

Pranav bought a yellow saree and wrapped it in a gift pack. The next day, He went to Aarohi's home to finish the formalities and thought of presenting it to her to apologize indirectly. He waited for a perfect moment when no one was around them.

"Aarohi... A small present for you," he slowly took out the gift and offered her.

Aarohi was quiet and upset.

"Take it. You'll love it."

She was still quiet.

"Look at this. It's your favorite color. I bought a saree in Yellow. It'll look perfect on you," he opened it himself as she wasn't putting her hand out to accept it.

As he was stepping forward, Aarohi began reacting in anger. "I don't want any gifts from you. You always give whatever you wish to. And later on, I should face the consequences. I neither need your gifts nor your compliments. Please take it back. And never present anything to me in the future."

He didn't understand what to do. After a while, he took the gift back to his hometown.

On the other hand, Aarohi started sharing her worries with Sara.

"Sometimes I don't feel like getting into this relationship, Sara. I don't think this wedding is the correct decision. He made a mistake, and he is blaming me for no wrong I did. I feel he is dominant. All of a sudden, he shouts at me. And right after that, he comes with a happy face. If he is angry, I should quietly face his wrath. If he is happy, I should merely maintain a smile. I should behave according to his mood. I don't want to get into all this. I don't even want to get married, Sara."

"If he is blaming you, then what are you doing, Aaru? You are also blaming his mistakes. After listening to your whole story, I feel there is also a mistake on your side. I agree that he should have informed you before not to reveal the ring. But after revealing it, you should have immediately informed Pranav when you felt a peculiarity in his mother's expressions. He could have taken care of it if you had informed him even before his family asked him out. After all this, he came to apologize by presenting a saree in your favorite color. But you didn't give him a chance."

"Did he come to apologize?"

"Yeah, Aaru. Why would he bring a saree in your favorite color? Try understanding him, Aaru. Sometimes people express intentions through their actions. You unnecessarily mistook him. Remember one thing, Aaru. If there is a mistake from his side, don't expect an apology. If there is a mistake from your side, don't wait to apologize. This is the key to a happy relationship. In a lifelong journey, You both shouldn't stop at a point counting each other's mistakes."

"I agree. I shouldn't have shouted at him, Sara. But what should I do now?"

"Call him, Aaru. Tell him that you are feeling sorry about what has happened."

"Will he accept my apologies? Or what if he takes a chance and always points out this mistake of mine?"

"Pranav doesn't seem like that, Aaru."

"How can you say that?"

"If he is a person of that kind, He would not have come all the way to apologize to you."

"I need some time, Sara," Aarohi said after a long pause.

The next day, Pranav was talking to Krishna.

"I did just as you said, Krishna. But she didn't understand my intention."

"Then put a full stop to all the misunderstandings and straight away say sorry to her, Kiddo."

"But..."

"Look, Pranav! When she says sorry, you should be sensible enough not to take her for granted. At the same time, When you say sorry, You should be confident enough that she won't take you for granted. The bond should be strong from both sides. If you are truly confident about her, apologize to her without a second thought."

"Pranav... the phone is ringing. Pick it up," Ratna shouted.

Pranav went to pick up the call.

In the meantime, Bhushan came to Pranav's home.

"Finally, you are here," Krishna was delighted.

"Yeah. Here I'm. How could I unfollow your orders," Bhushan laughed.

"Ok. Now follow this order as well. I don't want anyone to lose anything because of my family. So if you ever spend money on wedding arrangements, collect it from Pranav later."

"Don't worry, Krishna. Why would I spend money from my pocket? Pranav's money is already here with me. After finishing all the arrangements, I should only return him the balance amount."

"How come you have his money?" Krishna was confused.

NINE

LET'S MEET!

Pranav picked up the call.

'Pranav?'

'I'm sorry, Aarohi. I was unaware that you were hurt to this extent. I thought of making you happy by presenting a saree. But I think I've angered you more. I am still feeling bad about it.'

'No, Pranav. I am sorry for my rude behavior. You would have been hurt because of me.'

'Aarohi, I feel relieved now.'

'I too, Pranav.'

'I am out of guilt.'

'I too, Pranav.'

'I love you.'

'I too, Pranav.'

'Umm? Aarohi, Did you just say something?'

'Ah! You, too, said something.'

Both of them laughed.

'I feel like meeting you, Aarohi.'

'I too, Pranav.'

They laughed again.

'So, Where shall we meet? Shall I come to your place?'

'Yeah. But where?'

'Near tower clock?'

'Yeah. That would be fine, Pranav. And don't forget to get that Yellow saree. I liked it.'

'Hmm... You don't seem the way you are.'

Aarohi smiled.

'Okay. Just a couple of hours, and I'll be there.'

'Will be waiting for you.'

Pranav happily put off the receiver and turned back. Krishna was standing behind him.

'Hey, Krishna! What are you doing here?' Pranav asked Krishna.

'What are you... doing, Pranav?'

'What did I do?'

'A few months back, you acted in a stage show, right?'

'Yeah.'

'What is the name of it?'

'The groom is for sale.'

'What was it about?'

'It was to bring social awareness against dowry.'

'First of all, Are you aware of it?'

'What do you mean, Krishna?'

'Are we taking dowry from them?'

'Umm...Yeah,' Pranav slowly answered.

'"Practice what you Preach", Pranav. I know their financial condition. They couldn't afford it. Are we lacking money? Can't we live if we don't take money from them? Is this a marriage proposal or a business deal? They would have suffered badly for arranging the money. When I initially spoke with them, I told them that we don't need any dowry. I had confidence in you, Pranav. But you betrayed my trust. How can you even demand? Don't you have morals? I didn't even bring up this topic, as I completely believed you. Bhushan just told me that your dowry amount is with him. I immediately got enraged, Pranav.‘

’Stop it, Krishna. It’s not me. It’s your husband. I initially told him that I didn’t need a dowry. But Bhushan insisted on taking it. He was convincing. So I had to agree with him.‘

’If someone talks convincingly, Will you lose your values? Would you do whatever people suggest? If he suggests dropping out of this wedding, Will you do that? Shame on you, Pranav. Such an unbalanced behavior! You don’t have stability of mind. When someone gives you a suggestion, first think about whether it is correct or not. Stand on your decisions. Have a spine. I used to feel proud of you. But now I‘m scared,’ Krishna shouted and went away angrily.

Pranav was quiet.

After a couple of hours, Pranav reached the tower clock.

‘Hi, Aarohi! You are earlier than me,’ he wished Aarohi.

‘Look at this! I have brought the saree,’ he added.

‘Umm...Nice! Someone would have told you to ask about my favorite color. And someone else would have asked you to give a saree in the same color. You just took a yellow saree and came to me,’ Aarohi sighed.

‘What happened, Aarohi? Everything was fine between us, right?’

‘was... It was fine between us. But not now.’

Pranav was puzzled.

‘I heard everything in the call, Pranav.’

‘Damn! I didn’t press the receiver hard. This useless phone is making my problems bigger,’ Pranav spoke in his mind.

‘Come on, Pranav. Tell me. Maybe that "I love you", you said, might also be because of someone’s suggestion. Am I correct?'

'What the heck, Aarohi? If I follow someone's suggestion in one case, it doesn't mean whatever I do is because of the suggestions I get.'

'Stop protecting yourself, Pranav. I wouldn't have felt bad even if you decided to take dowry. But I'm furious that you are allowing someone to manipulate you. How could I put my life in your hands, Pranav? How could I live with a guy who has an instability of mind? How could I even believe any of your decisions in the future?'

'You are overthinking a lot, Aarohi. Only one mistake. And you are linking it to the past, present, and future. I was already feeling sorry about it. I was about to apologize to Krishna. But she went off in anger. I would have followed her to say sorry. But concidering that you would be waiting for me here, I had to start from my place immediately. But you... you only know overthinking and misunderstanding.'

'Am I... overthinking, Pranav?'

'Yeah. Before counting the negatives in me, first look into your mistakes. You just leave everything and start dreaming, Whenever there is a random conversation. Why do you overthink, Aarohi? You don't stop even there. You move a step forward, link everything to one particular scenario, and start blaming others.'

'Now, because I'm talking about your negatives, you are also digging my negatives, is it?'

'It's not me. It's you who started it, Aarohi. I at least accept my mistakes. But you don't even pay attention to my words.'

'Me? Huh. Remember our first phone call, Pranav? You said whatever you speak is from your heart. So you had all these in your heart. And you are now revealing your true colors.'

'Don't be rude, Aarohi. You are triggering me now.'

'I'm done, Pranav. I'm done with all of your stupidity. You always make mistakes and finally blame me. Even after all this, it's my mistake to still be here,' She turned back to return home.

'Go, Go back to your home. It is senseless to come to your hometown just to meet you. It's a waste of my time,' he shouted.

The very same day, he returned home tired and restless.

'Look at her, Pranav. Your sister has been shouting at me since the time you went out. You have returned, but she still hasn't stopped. She is making me feel that the one suggestion I gave has become the biggest mistake of my life,' Bhushan was sharing his concerns with Pranav.

'Leave it, Bhushan. It's my mistake, too. Aarohi was shouting at me regarding the same. It was a big battle over there.'

'Battle? Most of the fights are because of the lack of understanding. You know what, Pranav? There is a good quality in you. Even if it's late, you realize and accept your mistakes. In the same way, you might be having negatives too. No one in this world is an exception from imperfections. Aarohi might also have imperfections. So accept her imperfections, too, as you accept yours. While starting your life journey, there should be no misunderstandings or battles between you. There should be nothing except love. True love is beyond all these irregularities. In the purest relationship, you accept each other despite imperfections. You understand your partner to the extent that their peculiarities no longer trouble you.'

'But Bhushan, can I ask you something? Every girl dreams about sharing moments with her partner. Even my sister has such. But you would always be busy and don't spare time for her. How can you show your love to her when you can't even spend a minute with her?'

Bhushan laughed.

'Who said that I don't spend time with her, Pranav? When we were newly married, we went to a party. People over there made fun of Krishna, as I couldn't afford a better lifestyle for her. She never complained to me about it. But I wasn't able to leave her to all such insults. I started being strict in financial matters. I thought of working harder to give her a better life. I don't get time to travel along with her because of my busy schedule. But whenever I'm at home, I just put all my worries into the trash and start showering my love on her. How would you know the happenings at our home if you don't visit us at least once? This time, you should come along with Aarohi without a miss.'

'Now, what suggestions are you giving him, Bhushan? Are you again trying to spoil him?' Krishna shouted from the kitchen.

'No. No, Krishna. I'm just giving him a piece of useful advice,' Bhushan answered back.

Pranav and Bhushan laughed out loud.

TEN

'AARNAV' FOREVER

'Aarohi... Please pick up the call. Everyone in your home is picking up the call except you,' Pranav was trying to contact Aarohi. But she was hesitant to talk to him.

'Ok, now I'm left with only one option,' Pranav spoke to himself.

After three days, Aarohi got a parcel post from Pranav. There were three envelope covers and a gift pack in it. The envelopes were numbered. Aarohi first opened the first envelope.

Dear Aaru,

Right from my childhood, my home felt restricted. Whenever I was out, I used to chill out to the core. People thought I was a happy-go-lucky person until the count of my family turned from 4 to 3 and 3 to 2. Mom turned all her grief into temperament. Krishna got a new life, and I shifted all my focus to the business to forget all the pain. My life experienced several changes. In the flow of all these, I realized something. When dad was there, I never loved him.

I was always afraid of him. I was running away from him. I understood his care and affection for me only after he left us. I understood the value of a person only after a huge loss. I don't want to repeat the same mistake in my life. I want to live my life to the fullest along with you. I don't want to waste at least a second of my life with arguments and misunderstandings. I promise you that I'll make the correct decisions. I promise you to put all my ego aside when it comes to our relationship.

I am sorry for everything. I don't want to bring up the topic of our fight again. But let me tell you something.

If you are patient enough to misunderstand me all the time, I am patient enough too to clear all those misunderstandings. If you are patient enough to shout at me all the time, I am patient enough too to endure all of it. If you are patient enough to love me all the time, I am patient enough too to give back all the love in double. Life is short, Aarohi. Let's experience the purest love together. Let us not allow any of our imperfections to conquer our love. We are not Aarohi and Pranav anymore. We are Aarnav together. Love you, Aaru. I love you with all my heart.

This letter is not just a collection of letters.

It is an oath. It is an apology. It is a compilation of my heartbeats.

Lots of love,

Your better half!

'Aarnav?' She called out and smiled.

'I love you, too, Pranav. I can't express how happy I'm. To have you in my life is the best blessing I have ever got,' She spoke to herself in complete delight.

She then opened the second envelope.

It's a college admission letter. On looking at it, tears rolled out of her eyes.

'This... This letter is in my name. Can I still study?' She held the letter firmly and cried.

'Love of my mom and care of my dad. What else do I need, Pranav? I can do nothing in return but love and care just as you do.'

After a few minutes, she calmed down and opened the third envelope.

Solicit your gracious presence on the occasion of the marriage of

Mr. Pranav
(S/o. Late P.Subbaramaiah Chetty & Mrs. Ratnamma)

With

Ms. Aarohi
(D/o. Mr. C.Lakshmi Narayana Gupta & Mrs. Chandravatamma)

On Wednesday, the 3rd December 1997
at 10:15 AM at Arya Vysya Hostel, K.V street,
Madanapalli

Best compliments from:
P. Venkata Ramanaiah Setty & Sons
G. Naga Bhushanam & Krishnaveni

Will you marry me?

Aarohi's tears didn't stop.

She immediately made a phone call to Pranav.

'Aarohi?'

'Umm,' she slowly responded.

'You got the parcel?' Pranav asked.

Aarohi didn't say anything. She was just weeping in silence.

'Are you there?' he asked.

'Aarohi...' he called.

'Aaru...' he called again.

On hearing the word 'Aaru', she cried out loud.

'Aaru, Why are you crying?'

Aarohi still wasn't saying anything. Pranav was also not forcing her to speak. He was just waiting for her to cry her heart out and become relieved.

After a while, he slowly started calming her. 'Aarohi, now go and have a glass of water.'

'Umm,' She nodded and went.

She came back and began talking to him.

'It's a "Yes".'

Pranav smiled.

'Thanks for the love, care, and admission letter,' she smiled.

'Umm...Did you open the gift pack?' he asked.

'Not yet. But I know what it is. Saree, right?'

'Finally, it reached the right place,' he smiled.

'I am sorry, Pranav. I promise you that I will work on my negatives.'

'I promise that I will stop pointing out your negatives,' said Pranav

'I promise that I will stop talking rudely,' Aarohi added.

'I promise that I will control my anger,' Pranav said again.

'I promise you that I'll stop overthinking,' Aarohi continued.

'I promise that I'll understand you,' Pranav stressed it.

'I promise that I'll pay attention to your words before I word,' she assured.

'I promise that I'll stop all my lame jokes,' Pranav smiled.

'Nah! I don't want you to do that. They are my only relief,' Aarohi was playful.

Both of them laughed together.
'Aarohi..' Pranav slowly called her.
'Hmm?'
'Shall I say something?'
'Yeah, tell me.'
'May the love of Aarohi and Pranav remain forever.'
'Not "Aarohi and Pranav". It's "Aarnav" forever.'

Feeling like writing back to me?
preciselyinaccurate99@gmail.com

9 798889 862437

Printed by Libri Plureos GmbH in Hamburg,
Germany